Red Riding Hood

A Story About Bravery

Library of Congress Cataloging-in-Publication Data
Names: Rusu, Meredith, adapter. | Cuchu, 1977- illustrator.
Title: Red Riding Hood : a story about bravery / adapted by Meredith Rusu ;
   illustrated by Cuchu (Sònia González.)
Description: New York : Children's Press, an imprint of Scholastic, 2020. |
   Series: Tales to grow by | Summary: A retelling of the classic story
   emphasizing the role of bravery. Contains questions and guidelines for
   parents and educators.
Identifiers: LCCN 2019033811 | ISBN 9780531231883 (library binding) | ISBN
   9780531246221 (paperback)
Subjects: LCSH: Little Red Riding Hood (Tale)--Adaptations. |
   Wolves--Folklore. | Courage--Juvenile fiction. | Fairy tales. | CYAC:
   Fairy tales. | Folklore--Germany. | LCGFT: Fairy tales.
Classification: LCC PZ8.R8983 Re 2020 | DDC 398.2 [E]--dc23

Design by Book & Look.

Printed in North Mankato, MN, USA   113

1 2 3 4 5 6 7 8 9 10 R 29 28 27 26 25 24 23 22 21 20 ·

Scholastic Inc., 557 Broadway, New York, NY 10012.

Red Riding Hood

A Story About Bravery

Adapted by
Meredith Rusu

Illustrated by
Sònia González

Expert advice by
Eva Martínez

Children's Press®
An Imprint of Scholastic Inc.

In a quiet village, along a cobblestone path lined with ivy, stood a cottage. It was a happy home, with a bright flower garden and an even brighter young girl who lived there with her mother. The girl's name was Red Riding Hood.

She was called Red Riding Hood because of the hooded red sweater her grandmother had knit for her.

"You are so cheerful, my darling granddaughter," the old woman would say. "This cozy sweater matches the brightness of your heart."

Do you have a favorite outfit or piece of clothing? If so, what is it and how does it make you feel?

Red Riding Hood's grandmother would come every morning to help the young girl tend her mother's flower garden.

"Grandma, one day I want to have my own flower shop so I can sell daisies, because they're your favorite flowers!" Red Riding Hood would say.

Her grandmother would always smile. "And I'm sure one day you will."

Why did Red Riding Hood want to open her own flower shop? What would you like to be when you grow up?

Then, one morning, something odd happened. Red Riding Hood's grandmother did not come.

"Sweetheart, grandma is ill," said Red Riding Hood's mother. "She won't be able to visit today."

"Maybe a bouquet of her favorite daisies will help her feel better!" Red Riding Hood exclaimed.

"That's a wonderful idea," her mother said. "I will send you with some soup and bread as well. But you must promise to be careful on your way to grandma's cottage. There are wolves in the woods."

"I promise," said Red Riding Hood.

Soon, the young girl was skipping along the wooded path, holding a woven basket filled with goodies. No one could mistake her cheerful red sweater as she went.

Especially not the pair of wily eyes that spotted her through the trees.

What do you think Red Riding Hood felt as she brought the flowers to her sick grandmother? How would you feel in her shoes?

That child is the perfect plump morsel to fill my stomach, thought the big, bad wolf as he hungrily eyed Red Riding Hood. He rustled through the bushes, ready to pounce.

"Who's there?" Red Riding Hood called when she heard the noise. She remembered her mother's warning and grabbed a large stick to hold high.

Hmmm. This one has spunk, the wolf thought. *How much easier would it be to gobble her up if she were caught off guard? I'll bet she is taking that basket to the old woman in the cottage beyond the river. But I shall get there first!*

Quick as the wind, the wolf raced through the forest. Within moments, he was at grandmother's door.

"Who's there?" Grandmother asked when he knocked.

"It's Red Riding Hood," the wolf called, in a voice as gentle as the child's.

"My darling girl," Grandmother replied. "Come in—the door is unlocked."

When the old woman saw the ghastly wolf instead of her granddaughter, she fainted from shock. Quickly, the wolf hid her in a cupboard and put on her spare nightgown. Then, he closed the window curtains, climbed into bed, and pulled the sheets right up to his chin.

Soon, Red Riding Hood came skipping up to the door.
"Grandma, it's me!" she called.
"Come in," the wolf rasped.
Oh dear, Red Riding Hood thought. Her grandmother's
voice sounded strange. *She must be very ill.*

But when she entered the cottage, things only got stranger. The light was unusually dim. And her grandmother had the sheets pulled up to her chin.

"Grandma?" Red Riding Hood asked hesitantly.

Did Red Riding Hood feel safe entering the house?

Has someone ever looked different from how you remembered them? How did you react to the change?

"Come closer," the wolf whispered.

Red Riding Hood inched closer. "Grandma, you look different," she said. "What big eyes you have!"

"The better to see you with, my dear," replied the wolf. "If only you would come closer."

Red Riding Hood took another step. "But Grandma, what big hands you have!"

"The better to hug you with," whispered the wolf. He couldn't help grinning. Soon the child would be within reach—and soon after, in his belly.

As he grinned, the wolf's teeth flashed. And Red Riding Hood gasped. *What big teeth he has!* she thought. For by now, she could tell that this was not her grandmother at all, but a wolf like her mother had warned her about. She had to think fast or she would be eaten!

"Oh no, I completely forgot!" Red Riding Hood exclaimed. "I didn't bring your favorite flowers!"

"Don't be silly, child," said the wolf. "Come give your grandmother a hug."

"No, no," insisted Red Riding Hood. "Without your favorite flowers, you won't feel better. You remember which ones they are, right?"

Does Red Riding Hood's question about her grandmother's favorite flowers seem brave? Do you think asking questions can be brave?

Now the wolf paused. He didn't have the faintest idea which flowers were the old woman's favorite. But if he said so, the girl would catch on and run away.

"Fine, fine," rasped the wolf. "Go pick my favorite flowers, but then come right back."

Leaving her basket of goodies on the floor, Red Riding Hood raced out the door. But instead of fleeing back home, she crept around the back of the cottage to an open window. *Grandma must still be inside*, she thought. *And I must help her!*

Meanwhile, the wolf eyed the basket of treats. His stomach rumbled. *I have not eaten in three days,* he thought. *I suppose a small snack would do me well before the main course.*

Swiftly, the wolf devoured the treats. He was so busy munching, he never noticed the small girl in the red sweater sneak in the back window and free her grandmother from the cupboard.

When the bread was nothing but crumbs and the soup all gone, the wolf finally looked up. That was when he noticed the open cupboard and window.

"Wicked child!" he cried. "She escaped and took the old woman too! But I shall show them both what comes of trying to outsmart a wolf!"

Was the wolf brave for chasing Red Riding Hood and her grandmother?

The wolf sprang from the cottage. Now he was ravenous, not with hunger but with rage.

But so focused was he in his pursuit that he didn't pay attention to where he ran. He slipped on the slick stones by the river and tumbled down into the rushing water, never to be seen again.

Back in the village, Red Riding Hood told her mother the whole story.

"Thank goodness you are both safe!" her mother exclaimed. "But how did you outsmart that nasty wolf?"

"He couldn't tell me Grandma's favorite flowers." Red Riding Hood pressed a fresh bouquet of daisies into her grandmother's hand. "And I insisted I needed to pick some."

Think about times when you have been brave. What did people around you tell you? How did you feel?

"My darling girl," said Red Riding Hood's grandmother. "Now I see that your beautiful red sweater matches not only the brightness of your heart but the bravery within it as well."

What is bravery?

Bravery is the strength you need to try new things and face new challenges. Did you know that you have been brave ever since you were born? It's true! You've learned to walk, talk, explore, try new foods, or even say "no" to things you don't like. All of those required bravery!

What happens if I'm scared?

Sometimes, you might feel scared instead of brave. And that's okay. Fear is your body's way of telling you that something might be dangerous or "not right." Fear helps you to be careful. But even if you're scared, you can still be brave!

How do I feel brave instead of scared?

The best way to stop feeling afraid is to think about what's scaring you and *express* it. "Express" means to share. If you share what's frightening you with someone you trust, like a parent or teacher, you'll feel much better!

How can I express fear?

There are a lot of ways to do it!

- Draw what scares you the most and share it with adults around you.
- Use your words! Talk about your fear with someone you trust.
- Try building a play-dough sculpture of what's scaring you—and then squish it!

Continue being brave!

There are many different ways to show bravery every day. Here are just a few:

- In class, ask the teacher questions when there is something you don't understand.
- Say what you think, even if it's different from what your friends think. Just remember to use words that are kind, not hurtful.
- If a friend seems sad, ask them what's wrong. And then listen.
- If you see something that feels "not right," tell an adult.
- If you make a mistake, don't be embarrassed to talk about it. Everybody makes mistakes!
- Try a new dish or try to find a new friend. Being open to new things is brave too!
- And if it ever feels too hard to be brave, ask someone you trust for a very long hug!

You have achieved many things so far, thanks to your bravery. And you will accomplish many more!

GUIDELINES FOR FAMILIES AND EDUCATORS

Bravery is a natural motivator in every child. It's something we're born with in order to achieve our goals. As teachers and parents, we can promote bravery in our children so that they grow up with the idea that they are capable of doing amazing things, even when it's not easy.

Bravery involves exercising one's will in the face of an internal or external difficulty. When an obstacle appears, fear may appear as well. Fear is a natural emotion that makes children feel the need to protect themselves from danger. To ensure that fear does not prevent any child from carrying out their goals, we can help them with some guidelines:

- Let them make choices, even if they are wrong. Explain what the consequences of each choice will be, and allow them to assume the responsibility. This will strengthen their independence, but will also teach them that every choice has an outcome, good or bad. Managing small decisions is the first step to handling bigger ones.

- Encourage them when they succeed! Reinforce that they used bravery to do something amazing. And when they don't succeed, show your support. Let them know that you are confident they can do better next time. Your confidence in them now will become their own confidence in themselves in the future.

- Remind them often of their strengths. This will increase their self-esteem and help them rely on their own resources and strategies to achieve their goals.

• If they show fear, try not to downplay it by saying it is not real. Be their strength in the scary moments, even if the fear seems silly, and walk them through the steps of identifying what's scaring them, how it's affecting them, and what they can do to feel brave again.

• Discuss situations that are dangerous, and reinforce the need to be careful. Bravery is the positive management of fear, not the absence of it.

• When you see they cannot manage their fear, just hug them and show them love.

When we talk about emotions, there are no magic recipes. It takes time and care for children to learn to manage their emotions. And it's important for adults to offer support and trust. Children learn by example. If they see that we have confidence in them, then despite fear or difficulties, they will learn to trust that bravery will always come back and give them the strength to move forward.

Eva Martínez is a teacher and family counselor. She is the author of two books about emotional education for children, and she is a regular contributor to educational magazines in her native Spain.

TALES
To Grow By™

Enjoy the magic of fairy tales, and continue growing with more books in this series!

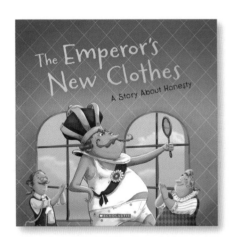

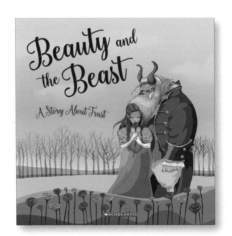